Sunny-Side Up

Beast opened the bag.

He held the egg up in the air.

"Out of the way, ants," Matthew yelled.

"Blast off," Richard shouted.

The egg hit the ground.

Beast and Matthew got down on their hands and knees.

"Ouch," Beast said. He looked at the knee with the scab. "Almost all off."

"It's not frying," Matthew said.

"No," said Richard. "And the yellow's all over the place."

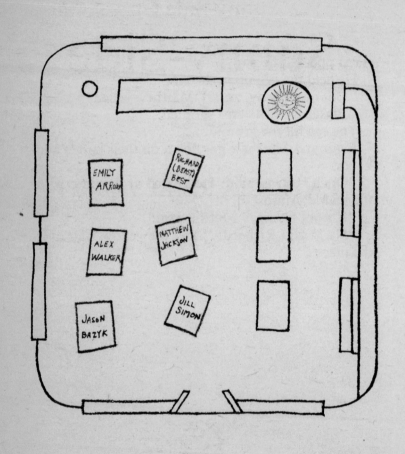

The Kids of the
11
Polk Street School

Sunny-Side Up

PATRICIA REILLY GIFF

Illustrated by Blanche Sims

Young Lions

With special thanks to John G. Peros

First published in the USA 1986 by
Dell Publishing Co., Inc.
First published in Great Britain 1988
in Young Lions
8 Grafton Street, London W1X 3LA

Young Lions is an imprint of the Children's Division,
part of the Collins Publishing Group

For Francis McHugh —
who moved away

Chapter 1

Beast looked out of the window.

It was going to be a hot day.

He reached under the kitchen table.

"Richard Best," his sister, Holly, said. "Did you stick your gum under there again?"

Beast didn't answer.

Last night's gum felt like a smooth, fat lump.

He pulled at it.

"MOTHER," Holly screamed. "Do you know what Richard has done again?"

Richard pushed his chair back.

He popped the gum into his mouth.

It tasted great. Cold and hard.

He made lots of teeth marks in it.

He kept opening his mouth wide.

Holly had to watch.

"Mother," she yelled again.

Richard turned and crashed through the green door. He ran across the lawn.

His mother poked her head out of the upstairs window. "Richard," she called.

He stopped.

"Where are you going?" she asked.

"To meet Matthew," he said.

He leaned over.

His jeans had a big hole in them.

He could see the scab on his knee.

He scratched it.

His mother said something else.

Maybe she had said, "Come back and make your bed."

He hoped not.

"What?" he yelled.

His mother said something else.

"See you later," he yelled.

He hurried down the street.

Matthew was standing on the corner.

He wasn't wearing jeans. He was wearing blue shorts.

"Why are you wearing shorts?" Beast asked.

Matthew's legs looked funny, he thought.

His knees were bony. Dirty too.

"My mother made me," Matthew said. "It's summer-time."

"You have a pool?" Beast asked.

"Nah," Matthew said. "Do you?"

Richard shook his head. He wished he had a pool. A great big blue one just like Emily Arrow's.

"Let's go and see Emily," he said.

"Good idea," said Matthew.

Beast ran ahead of Matthew.

He stopped at Linden Avenue.

He really wasn't supposed to cross alone, unless it was school-time.

But he was out of Ms Rooney's class now. Into Miss Gluck's.

He wasn't a baby any more.

9

He looked both ways.

Emily Arrow lived up the street.

He and Matthew went into her back garden.

Emily's pool was above ground. It took up most of the garden.

They climbed up the steps to look at the water.

"Too bad it isn't filled to the top," said Matthew. "If it was mine, I'd . . ."

Beast flicked a little water at Matthew.

"I'd fill it to the tippy top," Matthew said.

"I'd dive right in," Beast said.

"Can you swim?" asked Matthew.

"Under water," Beast said.

Matthew flicked a little more water at him. "I can float forever," he said.

Beast looked up at the house. "Looks like everyone is still asleep."

"I think this pool has a leak," Matthew said. "It's only filled halfway."

Beast nodded. "Maybe it's because of Stacey. Emily's little sister."

"Nah," Matthew said. "If you have a pool, you should fill it."

He climbed off the step.

"Where are you going?" Beast asked.

"To get the hose," Matthew said. "Fix this thing up a little."

Beast sat on the step.

He could hear someone yelling.

It sounded like Holly.

It sounded as if she were calling him.

Too bad.

He wasn't going to bother with her all summer.

He watched as Matthew hung the hose over the side of the pool.

"Turn the hose on all the way," Matthew said. "I hope Emily wakes up soon. We can get our bathing suits. Dive right – "

"It's going to be a great summer," Beast said. "The best."

Matthew shook his head. "It's going to be a terrible summer."

The back door opened.

They looked up.

It was Mrs Arrow.

"What are you doing?" she asked.

"Filling your pool a little," Matthew said. "I think you have a leak."

"I do not," Mrs Arrow said. "Turn off the hose."

"Is Emily up yet?" Beast asked.

"Yes," Mrs Arrow said. "But she's not here."

"Went to the beach?" Beast asked.

Emily was lucky, he thought. Double lucky.

A pool *and* the beach.

"She went to summer school," Mrs Arrow said. "It started today."

Beast looked at Matthew. "I forgot about that."

"Me too," said Matthew. "But I'm not going in these shorts."

"I don't blame you," Beast said.

Just then he heard Holly calling again.

She was down near Linden Avenue.

"Let's go," Beast said.

"You're in trouble, Richard," Holly yelled.

Beast rushed past her. "See you later," he told Matthew.

"You have to go to school," Holly said.

"I know, stupid," Beast said. "Where do you think I'm going?"

He hurried down the street. He turned the corner.

No one was in the school playground.

He was really late.

He raced across the playground and opened the door.

Chapter 2

Beast flew down the corridor.

"Those are school trousers?" a voice said.

He looked up.

It was Mrs Kettle, the strictest teacher in the school. "Just because it's summer-time . . ." she said. She shook her head.

Beast looked down at his jeans.

There were long strings hanging from the hole.

"I didn't know . . ." he began. "I forgot that . . ."

"Never mind," she said. "You're late."

Beast ran down the corridor.

He opened the door of Ms Rooney's room.

A couple of kids were standing at the blackboard.

A fat boy was sitting at Beast's desk. He had his thumb in his mouth.

Big baby.

Beast didn't know any of the kids.

He backed out again.

He wondered where he was supposed to go.

Maybe to Miss Gluck's room.

He stopped to think.

No, that was for September.

He looked around. Even Mrs Kettle was gone.

The corridor was empty.

He took a couple of sips of water. He swished them around in his mouth.

He was dying for an orange icedlolly.

He was dying to jump into Emily Arrow's pool.

He was sick of being in school for his whole life.

He was dying of the heat.

He stuck his head over the water fountain.

He ran a little over his hair.

Then he started to run down the corridor.

He jumped up to look in the windows. 110. 109. 106. 102.

Nobody.

He raced up the stairs.

Mrs Paris, his old reading teacher, was standing at the top.

"Hey, Beast," she said. "You don't look very happy."

"I hate school," he said.

Mrs Paris smiled. The lines around her eyes got deeper.

"I don't want to come here," he said.

"Listen, Richard," she said. "Sometimes things aren't so great. Like summer school."

He nodded.

"But you'll remember the good things about it."

He frowned a little.

"Wait and see," she said. "The children. The things you do."

She went past him. "I'm just going on holi-

17

day,'' she said. ''Going to the mountains.''

Richard walked down the corridor.

The door to Room 222 was open.

He looked inside. He saw Emily Arrow at the front desk.

Alex Walker was right behind her.

He saw Jill Simon too.

Beast stood there a minute.

He could see the teacher's back.

She was writing on the blackboard.

He wondered who it was.

She had long red hair.

Maybe it was someone new. Someone pretty.

She turned around.

Yucks.

She had fat cheeks like Jill Simon.

''Come in,'' she said when she saw him. ''I'm Mrs Welch.''

Beast slid into a seat next to Emily.

He looked around.

Counting him, there were only six kids.

He nodded at Jason Bazyk.

"Now," said Mrs Welch. "We are here to study reading."

She flicked back her hair. "And we'll do some writing too."

Richard sighed.

The sun was shining all over his desk.

He raised his hand.

Mrs Welch looked at him.

"Can I pull the blinds down?" he asked.

"Hurry up," she said.

Richard went to the side of the room.

He pulled the blind cord.

The blind sailed up to the top.

The whole thing rattled around.

The teacher shook her head.

She came over and pulled the blind down for him.

"Now," she said again. "Mrs Welch will tell about summer school."

Richard went back to his seat.

He put his hand in the desk.

Nothing in there.

No paper or anything.

He wished he had something to draw on.

Just then Matthew walked into the room.

He was wearing jeans.

Beast could see his blue shorts.

They were sticking out of the top of his jeans.

Matthew took a seat behind him.

"We're going to have arts and crafts," Mrs Welch said. "Make things. Really great things."

The teacher looked around. She smiled. "Place mats."

Emily Arrow raised her hand.

"We made place mats last year," she said. "In Ms Rooney's room."

The teacher frowned. "Well, we'll make something else."

She turned back to the board. "Right now we're going to do 'two vowels'."

"I know that," Emily Arrow said.

"You know a little too much," the teacher said.

Beast tried to remember the two-vowel thing.

He looked at the blind.

It was pulled down to the sill.

There wasn't one bit of air coming in.

He could hardly breathe.

The teacher came down the row. "You and . . . you," she said to Beast and Matthew. "Come to the front."

Beast followed Matthew to the front.

"Let's pretend . . ." the teacher began. She pushed Beast next to Matthew a little.

"I can't breathe in here," Jill said. She looked as if she were going to cry.

"Let's pretend you're two vowels." Mrs Welch said.

Beast looked at the floor.

He could see Emily beginning to laugh.

Matthew's face was all red.

The teacher wrote "Goat" on the board.

"You can be *O*," she told Beast.

"You can be *A*," she told Matthew.

Alex was laughing too.

"When two vowels go walking," said the teacher. "the first one does the talking."

She waved her hand. "Walk."

Beast and Matthew had to walk up and down.

"Stop laughing," the teacher told Emily and Alex. "Now talk," she told Beast.

Beast looked up at the ceiling. "Today is Monday," he said.

"See how easy," the teacher said. "Let's say it together."

Beast went back to his seat while everyone said the two-vowel rule.

Alex was pointing. "You're a vowel," he said.

Beast slid into his seat.

He leaned over to Matthew. "It's going to be a terrible summer," he said.

"I know," Matthew said. "But I know something even worse."

"What?" Beast asked.

Matthew looked up. "I'll tell you some other time."

Chapter 3

It was Thursday. The hottest day of the summer – so far.

Beast wiped his hands on his shirt.

Everything felt sticky.

Mrs Welch pulled the blinds down.

"You could fry an egg on the pavement," she said.

"Really?" asked Emily.

"Yucks," said Jill Simon.

Matthew and Beast looked at each other.

"I'd like to try that," Matthew said.

"Pass the salt," said Beast.

"And the pepper," Matthew said.

Mrs Welch smiled. "You two are always fooling around."

"Right," said Beast.

"Down to work now," Mrs Welch said. "Then arts and crafts."

She passed out some readers.

Old ones. Torn.

Richard wished Mrs Paris wasn't in the mountains.

She'd never give them messy books like that.

He looked at the print.

He crossed his eyes.

Everything on the page looked blurry.

Everyone read a sentence.

He counted down the page.

He'd have to read the fifth sentence.

He said the words to himself.

When Mrs Welch looked at him, he read aloud.

Perfect.

He shouldn't even be at summer school.

It was a big waste of time.

They read for a long time.

At last Mrs Welch told them to put their books away.

She passed out pieces of cloth. Each piece had little holes around the edges.

Beast got stripes. Brown and grey.

So did Matthew.

Emily got yellow flowers.

Jill got plain tan.

Jill looked as if she were going to cry.

"Want my stripes?" Beast asked.

She nodded. She passed him the tan cloth.

Then Mrs Welch passed out some long leather thongs.

They were stiff. Leathery.

"We're making wallets," Mrs Welch said.

"What for?" Beast said.

"To keep your money in," said Mrs Welch.

Beast felt in his pocket.

He had ten pence.

"I don't have any," Matthew said.

"Maybe you'll get some for your birthday," said Mrs Welch.

She showed them how to fold the cloth.

Then she told them to stick the thong through the holes.

"Go around the edges,"she said. She held up her wallet.

"That's great," said Emily.

Richard folded his cloth.

He dug the thong through it.

Then he looked at Matthew's.

Matthew's wallet was already a mess.

It had a big smear of something on it. Maybe jelly.

"Time's up," said Mrs Welch. "We'll do some more tomorrow."

Beast looked down at his wallet.

He had barely started.

There was a lot more time for reading than for arts and crafts.

"Get into line," Mrs Welch said.

Beast poked Emily Arrow. "Shall Matthew and I come over to your pool today?"

Emily put her cloth into her pocket. "Yes."

"I'll be there in three minutes," Beast said.

"Me too," said Matthew.

"Make that one minute," Beast said.

"Make it after lunch," Emily said. "I have to clean my room." She raced across the playground.

"Let's sit down a minute," Matthew told Beast.

They slid down against the playground fence.

"I'm going to tell you the terrible thing," Matthew said.

Beast looked at the fence.

He didn't want to hear about the terrible thing.

He bet Matthew had been kept back.

"Do you really think you could fry an egg on the pavement?" he asked.

Matthew shook his head. "I don't know."

"Did you get into trouble with the police?" Beast asked.

28

"Nah," Matthew said.

For a minute they watched a kid playing with a ball.

"Right after next week . . ." Matthew began.

"Just because you're a terrible reader . . ." Beast said at the same time.

They stood up.

"Not as bad as I used to be," Matthew said.

"Tell Ms Rooney," Beast said. "Tell her you're really going to work hard. Tell her I'll help you."

"You're a terrible reader too," Matthew said.

They walked through the playground and out of the gate.

Matthew bent over. He picked up a sycamore helicopter that had fallen from the tree.

He stuck it on his own nose.

He had to hold his head back to keep it there.

"I'm moving," he told Beast. "Moving away."

Richard swallowed. "Not kept back."

29

"You're never going to see me again," Matthew said. "Not around here. Not unless you come to Scotland."

Richard reached for a sycamore helicopter too.

He peeled it in half. "That's not so bad," he said.

But he knew it was bad.

It was terrible.

"You could have been kept back," he said.

"Yeah," Matthew said. "I'd still be here, though."

"It's not such a great place," Richard said. "I bet Scotland is better."

He didn't look at Matthew.

Scotland was probably terrible.

"I won't even finish summer school," Matthew said.

Beast pulled his sycamore helicopter apart.

"I'm going home now," Matthew said.

Beast watched him race down the street.

Then he started for home too.

31

Chapter 4

Richard ate lunch fast. As fast as he could.

He started for the door.

"Listen, Richard," Holly said. "Mother said you have to go to the shop."

"I will," Beast said. "On the way home from Emily's. Give me the money."

Holly gave him one pound. "Don't lose it. Get a box of macaroni and cheese."

"I hate that stuff." Beast stood on one foot. He stuck the money in his sock.

"Who cares?" Holly said. She looked out of the window. "Matthew Jackson is outside."

Beast raced out of the door. "Bye, Holly Lolly, the big fat Polly," he yelled.

"Hey, Beast," Matthew said. "You look funny in a bathing suit."

Beast looked down at his suit. "Why?"

"Your knees look funny."

Beast looked at his knees.

His scab was a big mess.

Half of it was coming off.

Underneath, his skin was shiny pink.

"Let's go," he said.

They hurried to Emily's house.

"I can hear splashing," Beast said.

They went up Emily's driveway.

"I'm as hot as anything," Matthew said. "I'm going to jump right into the water." He pulled off his trainers.

Emily poked her head out of the pool. Her hair was stuck to her head. "Wash your feet in the bowl."

Beast pulled off his trainers too.

He put his pound under a rock.

He waited until Matthew jumped out of the bowl. Then he jumped in.

The water was warm from the sun. Pieces of

grass floated around in it. Some of them stuck to his ankle.

Matthew climbed the pool ladder. He held his nose. "Come on, Beast," he said.

Beast gave Matthew a little push.

Matthew splashed in.

Then he held his own nose. "Banana dive," he shouted. He jumped in.

His feet touched the bottom.

He opened his eyes.

They burned a little.

He could see Matthew's legs. He could see Emily's orange bathing suit.

They were all wavery.

He popped his head up.

"Yeow!" Matthew was yelling. "It's cold."

"Freezing," Beast said.

"It's good when you get used to it," Emily said.

She lay on her back. "I can float. Look."

"I can only do that on my stomach," Beast said.

"Goodbye," Matthew said. "I'm going to swim under water."

Beast held on to the side of the pool. He looked up at the sky.

He felt warm, wonderful.

Emily came over next to him.

"Your eyelashes are stuck together," he told her. "They look like stars."

Matthew poked his head up. He took a deep breath. Then he dived down again.

Emily's mother came out. "I'm leaving fruit juice," she said. She put three glasses on the back steps.

Beast let his legs float up. "Summer is the best," he said.

Matthew's head popped up. "Count!" he yelled.

He dived down again.

Beast started to count.

Emily climbed the ladder. "I'm getting my juice," she said.

"Eighteen . . .nineteen," Beast counted. "Twenty . . . twenty-one."

Matthew raised his head. "How long?"

"Twenty-two," Beast said. "Almost."

Matthew held on to the side of the pool too. "Have to get my breath," he said.

"Isn't the summer the best?" Beast said.

Matthew nodded.

"I love Emily's pool," Beast said.

"And the juice," Matthew said.

Beast looked at his fingers. They were starting to shrivel up.

Then he thought of Matthew's terrible news.

He could see Matthew was thinking about it too.

"I wonder if they have pools in Scotland," Matthew said.

"Of course they do," Beast said. "I bet they do."

He wondered if they had juice in Scotland.

Matthew kicked his feet. "I'm getting out now," he said. "I'm going to get my juice."

Beast nodded. "I'm coming in a minute."

He looked up at the sky again. He remembered Ms Rooney said not to look at the sun.

Instead he looked at a cloud.

He wondered if the same cloud was hanging over Scotland.

He sighed. Scotland was far away.

Almost as far as the cloud.

He started to climb out of the pool. He was getting cold.

Chapter 5

Beast yawned.

He hated to get out of bed.

"What day is it?" he called out.

"Saturday," his mother called back.

"Don't you even know that?" Holly yelled.

Beast felt wide awake.

He jumped out of bed.

It was as hot as anything.

He could hear the bees buzzing outside.

They were probably hot too.

He threw on his bathing suit.

He went down to the kitchen.

"Can we go to the beach today?" he asked his mother.

She shook her head. "Too much to do. This place is a mess."

He grabbed a bunch of grapes.

"Eat your cereal," his mother said.

He reached into the Sugar Puffs box. He took a handful.

Then he went outside.

It was a beach day.

A swimming day.

Maybe he should go over to Emily Arrow's.

Then he remembered.

Emily was at her aunt's house today.

Her aunt probably had a pool.

Maybe it was even bigger than Emily's.

Emily was a lucky kid.

He saw Matthew coming down the street.

Matthew grinned at him. He held out a brown paper bag.

"Look what I've got," he said.

Richard reached for the bag.

Inside was an egg.

It was a brown one.

"I've had my breakfast," he told Matthew.

"No." Matthew shook his head. "I took it to fry. To see if it works."

"Like Mrs Welch said?" Richard asked. "On the pavement?"

"I tried to get two," Matthew said. "But this was the last one."

"What about the school playground?" Richard said.

"Nah," Matthew said. "It's Saturday. Probably all locked up." He looked around. "Maybe right here. On the pavement."

Beast shook his head. "Holly will be out any minute. Spying."

"In the park," Matthew said. "Near Linden Avenue."

Richard bent down to scratch his scab.

It was very itchy.

Then he looked up. "It won't work. No pavement there."

Just then, Holly came out.

She walked down the path.

"What are you doing now?" she said.

Richard closed the bag. "Mind your own – " he began.

"I'm going to Joanne's house," Holly said. "Don't try to follow me."

She started across the street.

"What a pain," Beast said.

He waited until she was gone.

"I know a great place," he said. "In the garage."

They walked around to the back of the house.

Beast pushed open the doors.

"Nobody ever goes in here," he said. "It's a big wreck."

They stood at the doorway looking in.

Beast's old Big Wheels was in front.

Then there was Holly's doll's pram. It was lying on its side.

There were tools.

There was a ladder.

There was an old Happy Families game.

The Happy Families cards were all over the floor.

"Wow," Matthew said. "You have a lot of stuff."

"Great, isnt' it?" Beast said.

Matthew shook his head. "We can't fry an egg in here."

"Right in front," said Beast. "In a sunny spot. Holly's gone. My mother's upstairs."

Beast opened the bag.

He held the egg up in the air.

"Out of the way, ants," Matthew yelled.

"Blast off," Richard shouted.

The egg hit the ground.

Beast and Matthew got down on their hands and knees.

"Ouch," Beast said. He looked at the knee with the scab. "Almost all off."

"It's not frying," Matthew said.

"No," said Richard. "And the yellow's all over the place."

"It's supposed to stay in one round thing," Matthew said.

"Not always," Richard said.

Suddenly he looked up. "Hey, Matthew. I've just thought of something."

Matthew stuck his finger in the edge of the egg. "Not even getting hot."

"Listen, Matthew," Richard said. "You don't have to move. I've just thought of a great idea."

He gave his knee another scratch. "It's the greatest idea I've ever had."

Chapter 6

"Today is Wednesday," Mrs Welch said. "A writing day."

"Is it a wallet day too?" Jill Simon asked. Her fingers were crossed.

"We'll see," said Mrs Welch.

Richard looked around for some paper.

He saw that Matthew was looking too.

"It's easy to forget in the summer-time," said the teacher. "I'm giving paper out."

She pulled some paper out of her desk.

"You're the paper monitor," she told Alex. "Give out one for scrap. One for good."

Alex slapped two pieces on Beast's desk.

It was the yellow kind. The kind with the light blue lines.

Richard hated it.

It made his writing look fuzzy.

His rubber always made holes in it.

The teacher stood at the blackboard. She picked up a piece of chalk. "Mrs Welch is going to show you friendly letters," she said. "It's important."

Beast slid down in his seat.

The only time he'd ever written a letter was last year.

It was to his Aunt Anne.

He had to thank her for the birthday underwear.

Mrs Welch wrote "Polk Street School" up in one corner.

She wrote "Polk Street" underneath.

Then she put the date: 8 July.

"Psst," said Emily. "Want to come in my pool today?"

Beast frowned. He shook his head.

"Why not?" Emily whispered.

"Mrs Welch doesn't like talkers," Mrs Welch said.

Emily kept looking at Beast.

He pretended he hadn't seen her.

Then Emily put her nose up in the air.

He knew she was cross with him.

He sighed. He'd have to tell her.

Mrs Welch wrote "Dear Scott" on the other side of the board.

Beast leaned over.

"It's about an egg," he told Emily.

Mrs Welch turned round.

Beast pretended he was scratching his knee.

The teacher clicked her teeth. Then she turned back to the board.

"The egg smashed in front of the garage," he said. "I have to clean it up. I have to stay in the garden all day."

He picked up his pencil.

He was dying to draw something.

Maybe he could use his scrap paper.

He'd make his friendly letter right the first time.

He began to draw a big blue pool.

He drew himself diving in the water.

"Splesh," he wrote underneath.

"Now," said Mrs Welch. "The rest is easy."
She began to write wavy lines under "Dear
Scott".

"Mrs Welch wants you to write your own letter," she said. "Tell about the summer."

Richard reached for his scrap paper.

Just then Matthew tapped him on the back.

He looked over his shoulder.

"I'm coming over today," Matthew said. "I'll
bring some stuff."

Richard nodded. "Great, Matthew," he said.

Maybe Matthew would help him clean up the
egg stuff.

He picked up his pencil again.

He drew Holly trying to swim.

She looked as if she'd drown any minute.

"Glub, glub," he said.

"Let's get going," said Mrs Welch.

Beast reached for his good paper.

"Polk Street School," he wrote at the top.

"DEAR SCOTT."

Matthew tapped him again. "I'm bringing a tin of peas," he said.

"I hate peas," Richard said.

"Me too," said Matthew. "But it was the only thing I could get."

Richard picked up his pencil again.

Then he started to write:

I hope you are having a grate summer. I am having a grate summer.

My frend was almust moving moving away. But I have a plan.

Your friend,
Richard Best

Chapter 7

Richard scraped up the egg.

Behind him, Matthew made gagging sounds.

Beast wanted to make gagging sounds too.

"This stuff is really stuck on here," he said.

"Want me to help?" Matthew said.

Beast shook his head. "It's all right?" he said.

Matthew opened the garage doors.

"Smells cool," he said. "Like my cellar."

Beast threw the egg mess behind a bush.

He went into the garage too.

"It'll be a great place for you, Matthew," he said.

Matthew nodded. He held up an old blue rug.

It had balls of dust on it.

He shook it a little.

"I can use this," he said. "For my living room."

Beast pushed an iron pipe out of the way. "Here's your bedroom. Right here at the back."

Then he saw a spider.

It was spinning a web in Matthew's bedroom.

Beast pushed it with his hand.

He didn't want Matthew to see it.

Maybe Matthew was afraid of spiders.

He sat down on Holly's old doll's pram.

"Here's the kitchen," Matthew said. He pointed with his foot. "I'll keep my peas right up here. Save them for the winter."

Then he frowned. "It's going to be cold."

Richard, tried to think of something to say.

"Not so bad," he said after a minute.

"I'll need a blanket," Matthew said. "Maybe you could . . ."

Beast thought of his red blanket.

It was puffy.

Warm.

He loved it.

He didn't answer.

"Let's tell Emily about this place," Matthew said. "Tell her I'm going to run away and live here."

Beast nodded. "She'll love it."

"Maybe she can get some food too," said Matthew.

"Don't worry," Beast said. "I'll save you some stuff. School lunch."

Matthew looked worried. "I hope it's enough. I love to eat."

Just then Beast heard Holly.

She was talking to her friend Joanne.

He jumped off the doll's pram.

He dived for the garage doors.

He shut them just in time.

Holly was coming up the driveway.

"Ssh," he told Matthew.

They tiptoed to the window.

The window was dusty.

They could hardly see.

Beast rubbed it.

Holly and Joanne sat on the grass. "I wish we had a pool," Holly said.

"She wants everything," Beast whispered. "Even my mother says so."

Matthew tapped on the glass a little.

"Don't do that," Beast said.

"She'll think it's a ghost or something," Matthew said.

He tapped again.

Holly jumped.

Beast and Matthew started to laugh.

They ducked away from the window.

"Holly's scared of everything," Beast said.

"Is that you in there?" Holly shouted. "Is that you, Richard?"

"It's that stupid boy and his friend," she told Joanne.

"Come on," Joanne said. "We'll go over to my house."

"Right," Holly said.

"Whooo," Matthew said.

Richard started to laugh again.

He fell over the doll's pram.

He stopped laughing and pulled his leg up.

His knee was bleeding.

He'd have another scab tomorrow.

He swallowed hard and blinked.

"You're crying," Matthew said.

"I am not," Beast said.

"It's okay to cry," Matthew told him. "My father said so."

"I'm not crying," Beast said again.

"Even my father cried once," Matthew said. "I saw him."

Beast looked up. "Really? When?"

"When my grandfather died."

Richard nodded. He stood up.

His knee was stinging.

"It's all right now," he said. "It just hurts a little."

He went over to Matthew's kitchen. "I'm going to get you a fork and everything."

Matthew grinned. "You're my best friend," he said. "You've saved me from going to Scotland."

Beast grinned back. "You're my best friend too."

He thought for a minute.

"Listen, Matthew," he said. "You can have my red blanket."

Matthew ducked his head. "Great," he said.

They heard Holly and Joanne walking down the driveway.

"If my mother finds out Richard is in the garage . . ."Holly said.

"You should tell," Joanne said.

Beast looked at Matthew.

They didn't say anything for a minute.

"I hope she doesn't," Beast said. "I hope she doesn't spoil everything."

Chapter 8

Beast pushed the thong into the tan cloth.

His wallet was looking good.

Even Mrs Welch said so.

She was walking up and down the row.

''Two minutes more,'' she said. ''Then we'll do 'two vowels' again.''

Alex looked at Beast.

He started to laugh.

Beast looked down at his wallet.

He knew what Alex was thinking.

Matthew tapped his shoulder. ''I hope we don't have to do the walking.''

''Me too,'' Beast said.

Mrs Welch went to the front of the room. She wrote three words on the board.

    1. t*ai*l

2. g*oa*t

3. str*ea*m

"Write these words in a sentence," Mrs Welch said. "First one finished gets a prize."

Beast grabbed a piece of paper.

He looked up at the board.

Tail.

"Taaaaal," he said to himself.

Easy.

"THE CAT HAS A TAIL."

He looked up again.

Goat.

He knew it from last time.

"THE GOAT SAYS BAAA."

The third one was the hardest.

He looked at it.

Str – eeee – m.

He couldn't think of a sentence.

Kites have streamers, he thought.

Quickly he wrote, "THE KITE HAS A STREAMer."

He rushed to the front of the room.

Emily rushed to the front too.

Mrs Welch looked at their papers. ''Two prizes,'' she said.

She handed a little packages to Beast.

She gave one to Emily too.

There was a picture of a carrot on Beast's. And a word: *SEEDS*.

''Two vowels in seeds,'' said Mrs Welch.

Beast looked across at Emily's package.

Emily had a picture of a beetroot.

''Plant these seeds,'' Mrs Welch said. ''You'll have nice vegetables.''

Beast raced back to his seat.

''We'll plant them today,'' he whispered to Matthew. ''For you. For food.''

Emily looked across the row.

''Want my beetroot?'' she asked. ''I hate beetroot.''

''I'm not crazy about beetroot,'' he said. ''I'll take them, though.''

"Time to go home," said Mrs Welch.

"I'll be over later," said Emily. "I'll help you plant them."

Beast nodded. "We want to tell you something too."

He and Matthew headed for his house. They went straight to the garage.

"There's a great spot back here," Beast said. "Behind the garage. Even Holly won't see it."

They dragged a shovel out.

Then they pulled the hose around.

Matthew started to dig.

"Tough," he said. "Lots of rocks and stuff."

"We've got to do it, Matthew," said Beast. "You have to eat."

"Right," said Matthew. "I love carrots. Beetroot too."

At last they had a little patch cleared.

"Good enough," Matthew said. He wiped his forehead.

They dumped the seeds on the spot.

Beast put a clump of dirt on top.

Then Matthew turned on the hose.

Just then Emily came up the driveway. "Hey," she said.

Emily was wearing a green bathing suit today.

She was dripping wet.

"Were you in the water?" Beast asked.

He was as hot as anything.

"I stopped for a quick dip," Emily said.

"Lucky," he said.

"Too bad you couldn't come over," she said.

They walked around to the garage.

"I'll tell you a secret," Matthew said.

Emily leaned over.

"I'm going to live here," Matthew said. "Forever."

Emily looked around. "In Beast's house?"

Matthew shook his head. "In the garage."

"Here?" Emily asked. "In this dirty old garage?"

"We're fixing it up," Beast said.

"Why?" Emily asked.

"I'm supposed to move," Matthew said. "To Scotland."

"That's terrible." Emily looked as if she wanted to cry. "We'll never see you again."

"That's why he's going to live here," Beast said.

Emily shook her head a little.

"Without any lights?" she asked.

"Yup," Matthew said.

"And no television?"

Matthew swallowed.

"Without your mother?" she asked. "And your father? All alone? In the night-time?"

Matthew sat down on the rug. He didn't say anything.

"It's going to be cold too," Emily said.

"I never thought of that," Matthew said.

"I'm lending you my blanket," Richard said. "Remember? The red puffy one."

Matthew shook his head. "No. I meant my mother and father."

"And Christmas," Emily said.

Beast frowned at her. "We're going to have great times," he said. "Matthew and me. We'll do lots of things."

He kept watching Matthew.

Matthew was crying now. "I have to go home now," he said.

"I'll give you my pillow too," Beast said. "And one of my Christmas presents. No. More than one."

But Matthew didn't answer him. He started down the driveway.

Beast went after him. "Half," he yelled. "Half my presents."

He watched until Matthew turned the corner.

Chapter 9

It was Thursday again.

Beast didn't have to go to summer school today. His mother had let him stay at home. Matthew was leaving today.

Beast sat on the steps in front of Matthew's house.

There was a huge red truck in the driveway.

Beast stretched out his legs.

The steps were too warm to lean against.

He watched a bumblebee flying around Matthew's bushes.

They weren't Matthew's bushes any more.

Now they belonged to a boy named Joseph Ohland.

Matthew had told him so.

Just then, Matthew came out of the house. His

brothers and sister came out too.

Matthew was wearing brown trousers and a red shirt.

He looked hot. He looked funny in grown-up trousers.

He was carrying a GI Joe truck.

One of the wheels was missing.

He dumped it on Beast's lap.

"I can't take this with me," he said. "My mother said it's a wreck."

"I'll take it," Beast said. "I'll save it for you. Right in your living room."

"In case I ever come back," Matthew said.

"Right,"

Just then, Matthew's mother and father came down the steps.

Mrs Jackson looked hot too. "Time to go," she said.

"I'll never see you again," Beast said.

"I know," Matthew said.

"No," Mrs Jackson said. "We'll invite Beast for a visit."

Beast reached into his pocket. "Here's my wallet, Matthew," he said. "With ten pence."

Matthew nodded. "It's the best."

"Want a ride?" Matthew's father asked. He opened the car door. "We'll drop you off at your house."

Richard piled into the back seat with Matthew and his brothers.

In front of them the big moving van began to move.

Beast nudged Matthew. "Hey, look . . ." he said.

Matthew grinned. "Easy Moving Truck."

"Two vowels," said Beast.

"Right," said Matthew.

They stopped at the light.

Beast could see Emily coming home from summer school.

Jill Simon was with her.

She waved at them. "Goodbye, Matthew," she shouted.

"See you, Matthew," Jill yelled.

"See you," he yelled back.

They passed the A&P store at Linden Avenue.

Matthew nudged him. "Look at all those peas in the window."

Beast swallowed. "I still have your peas," he said.

"Save them," Matthew said. "Eat them if you want to."

Beast nodded.

They pulled up at Beast's front door.

"Can Matthew come with me?" Beast said. "Just for a minute."

Mr Jackson looked at his watch. "Only for a minute," he said.

Matthew jumped out of the car.

They went around to the garage.

"I want to show you," Beast said.

Matthew looked.

A little mass of green was coming up through the dirt.

"Carrots" Matthew said. "Beetroot too. I love them."

"Right," said Beast.

He walked Matthew back to the front.

"Listen, Matthew," Beast said. "Mrs Paris said something."

Matthew looked at him.

"She said when things weren't so great, I'd remember the good stuff."

Matthew opened the car door. He nodded.

Mr Jackson started the motor.

Matthew slid inside.

Beast had to raise his voice.

He wanted to be sure Matthew heard him.

"I'll remember the two vowels," he said.

Matthew looked back. "I'll remember the egg on the pavement," he yelled.

"And your kitchen," Beast yelled.

"I'll write you a friendly letter," Matthew shouted. "Tonight."

Beast watched the car go down the street.

"I'll write to you too," he shouted.

He wasn't sure if Matthew could hear him any more.

Then the car turned the corner.

Beast listened to the sound of the motor.

Then he couldn't hear it any more.

"I'll remember you, Matthew," he shouted.

He was crying.

He was glad Matthew's father had said it was all right to cry.

He knew Matthew was crying too.

He went back up the driveway.

He stopped to look in the garage.

He'd never eat the peas.

He was going to leave them there forever.

The Reluctant Dragon

KENNETH GRAHAME

'I *can't* fight and I *won't* fight. Besides, I haven't an enemy in the world,' the dragon announced firmly.

And he did so want a peaceful life. To write sonnets and find a place in Society was all he asked. So why did the whole town insist that he battle with St George, who was such a nice fellow anyway?

The Paddington Books
MICHAEL BOND

Paddington is a *very* rare bear indeed! He'd travelled all the way from darkest Peru (with only a jar of marmalade, a suitcase and his hat) when the Brown family first met him on Paddington Station. Since then their lives have never been quite the same . . . for things just seem to *happen* to Paddington – chaotic things.

What *other* bear could turn his friend's wedding into an uproar by getting the wedding ring stuck on his paw? Or glue himself to his dancing partner's back with his marmalade sandwich? *Only* Paddington . . . but as he says himself, 'Oh dear, I'm in trouble again.'

'Within a comparatively short time, Paddington has joined Pooh as one of the great bears of children's literature.'   *The Teacher*

Paddington's own particular brand of chaos comes up often in Young Lions – in *A Bear Called Paddington*, *More About Paddington*, *Paddington Goes to Town*, *Paddington Helps Out*, *Paddington at Large*, *Paddington Abroad*, *Paddington Takes the Air*, *Paddington Marches On*, *Paddington at Work*, *Paddington on Top*, *Paddington Takes the Test*, *Paddingtons Blue Peter Story Book* and *Paddington on the Screen*.

The Boy Who Sprouted Antlers

JOHN YEOMAN AND QUENTIN BLAKE

'As long as you set your mind on it and try hard enough, there's nothing you can't do,' said Miss Beddows to Billy when he declared that he simply couldn't make a basket. Billy liked the idea that he could do anything, but Melanie and Paul didn't agree.

'What about growing horns?' said Melanie. It was a challenge that Billy had to accept.

'Wildly improbable and cleverly sustained.'   *Margery Fisher*

Hilarious reading for sevens and up.

The Gingerbread Rabbit

RANDALL JARRELL

One day as a mother was gazing out of her window, she saw the biggest, brownest rabbit in the garden.

'What a pity,' she said, 'he won't be here for my little girl to see.'

But the big brown rabbit gave the mother an idea. Back in the kitchen, she got out some flour and treacle and brown sugar and ginger, and made a big, brown, gingerbread rabbit for her little girl. Then, just as she was about to put him in the oven, he wriggled out of her hands and ran out of the house into the forest. That was the beginning of the rabbit's and the mother's adventures.

This delightful story is just right for those who can now read for themselves.

Simon and the Witch

MARGARET STUART BARRY

Simon's friend the witch lives in a neat, semi-detached house with a television and a telephone, but she has never heard of Christmas or been to the seaside. However, she has a wand, which she loses, causing confusion at the local constabulary, and a mean-looking cat called George, who eats the furniture when she forgets to feed him. The witch shows Simon how to turn the school gardener into a frog, and she and her relations liven up a hallowe'en party to the delight of the children and the alarm of the local dignitaries. With a witch for a friend, Simon discovers, life is never dull.

Very highly recommended by ILEA's *Contact* magazine: '. . . who could resist such a lively character?'

You will find more adventures of Simon and the Witch in *The Return of the Witch*, *The Witch of Monopoly Manor* and *The Witch on Holiday*, all in Fontana Lions.

The Ice Palace

ROBERT SWINDELLS

Far away in the lands of the north, in the village near the dark forest, all the people lived their lives in fear and great sorrow. For every night the evil Starjik would round up his wolves and come to steal away yet another child from the village. But when Ivan's little brother disappears, he is determined to find him, and sets off on a long and perilous search through the frozen wastes.

Suspense, excitement, extreme human courage and a strange winter landscape combine in this lovely fantasy tale that will involve the reader from the first moment.

Pat Ross

Pictures by Marylin Hafner

Meet M and M
M and M and the Bad News Babies
M and M and the Haunted House Game
M and M and the Mummy Mess

Best friends Mimi and Mandy have a whole host of adventures in these stories.

They go shopping by themselves. They get their first babysitting job. They dress up in spooky costumes and end up getting a fright themselves. And they go in for some do-it-yourself mummy wrapping at the natural history museum.

Wonderfully illustrated stories for the beginner reader.